# Ghost Rescue

## AND THE
## HOMESICK MUMMY

# Ghost Rescue

## AND THE
## HOMESICK MUMMY

WRITTEN BY
**Andrew Murray**

ILLUSTRATED BY
**Sarah Horne**

ORCHARD BOOKS

ORCHARD BOOKS
338 Euston Road, London NW1 3BH
*Orchard Books Australia*
Level 17/207 Kent Street, Sydney, NSW 2000
First published in hardback in Great Britain in 2009 by Orchard Books
First published in paperback in 2009
ISBN 978 1 84616 352 4 (hardback)
ISBN 978 1 84616 360 9 (paperback)
Text © Andrew Murray 2009
Illustrations © Sarah Horne 2009
A CIP catalogue record for this book is available from the British Library.
1 3 5 7 9 10 8 6 4 2 (hardback)
1 3 5 7 9 10 8 6 4 2 (paperback)
Printed in Great Britain
Orchard Books is a division of Hachette Children's Books,
an Hachette UK company.
www.hachette.co.uk

"Lord Fairfax?" said Charlie.

"Yes, Charlie?" said his ghostly friend. "What's on your mind?"

"When did you and your family live — your wife, and Florence, Zanzibar and Rio? I mean, how long ago? And what did you do?"

"Well, Charlie," said Lord F, "it was seventy years ago, and we had Fairfax Castle to look after... But I loved ancient Egypt, and sometimes I went there, to the sun and sand and the River Nile, to dig in the Valley of the Kings. Goodness! It seems such a long time ago..."

Then there was a beep.

"You have email," said the computer.

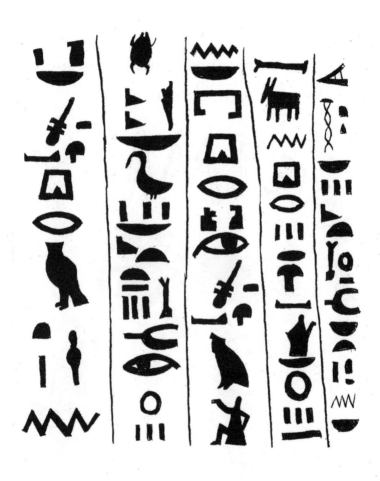

"What on earth is this?" asked Charlie.

"Charlie!" Lord F exclaimed in excitement. "This email is in ancient Egyptian hieroglyphics! Now, what does it say?"

He put on his ghostly reading glasses and frowned at the screen.

He peered and pondered, and then translated slowly to Charlie, who typed it all up.

Deer Toast Rascal,
Elf!
I am a dummy, and I am a parsnip in the E shipped Marzipan. Fleas can you elf me? It's sew coal in this candy! I just ant to go hum to E shipped. I lung for the sin and spam – but eggs petrolly I ant to be WORM!
Minitap

Lady F and Florence came in, and they all stared at the translation.

"Oh, Reginald," scolded his wife. "This is complete nonsense! You really are rusty. You'll need to brush up your Egyptian if we're to find out what this really says—"

"Wait a minute," Charlie interrupted. "It's nonsense…but it seems so close to making sense. 'Deer'…well, that must be 'Dear', and 'Toast Rascal' sounds like…'Ghost Rescue'! Only a mummy would write to us in hieroglyphics, so the 'dummy' must be a 'mummy'…"

"I do believe you're right!" smiled Lord F. "Carry on!" And soon they had come up with this:

Dear Ghost Rescue,
Help!
I am a mummy, and I am a prisoner in the Egypt Museum. Please can you help me? It's so cold in this country! I just want to go home to Egypt. I long for the sun and sand — but especially I want to be WARM!
Menhotep

Charlie put a piece of the Fairfax Castle foundation stone in his pocket, so the ghosts could come with him. Then he went out to the Ghostmobile, which was an old pizza delivery van, parked in the lane behind his house. Charlie got into the driver's seat (phew, it still smelled of garlic).

He slid down so he could press the pedals with his feet, and reached up to turn the steering wheel. The ghosts acted as his eyes and ears.

It was night when they reached the Egypt Museum. The place was dark and quiet. Charlie would have to break in, like a common burglar. He had done this before in the cause of rescuing ghosts. But even though the Fairfaxes were keeping a lookout for him, he was very nervous. He checked a window for burglar alarms, and forced it open. His heart drummed in his ears and his hands dripped with sweat.

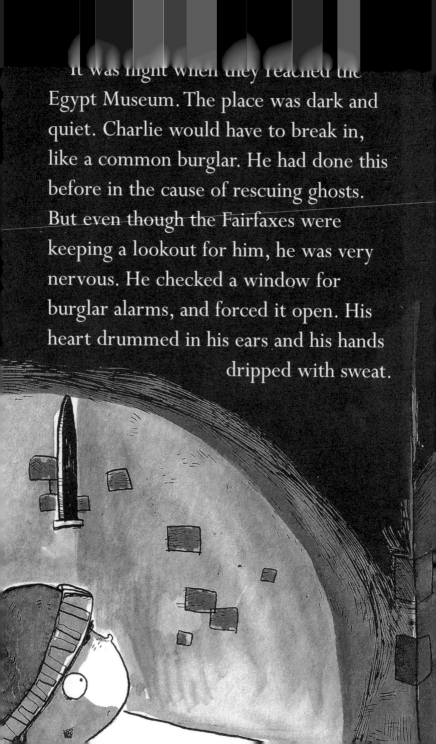

"What was that noise?"

"Just a fox in the bushes, Charlie."

Then Charlie was inside, and the ghosts drifted in with him.

PIZZA

It was a dark, spooky place. Weird shadows loomed up around Charlie's torch, and Charlie had to remind himself that they were just statues of gods and pharaohs. Where was the mummy who had called for Ghost Rescue?

None of the ghosts had any idea – until Zanzibar caught a scent.

"Wwrruff?"

Ahead was a faint orange glow. And there they found him, not a rotting mummy at all, but the ghost of an Egyptian. He wore a smart tunic, sandals and headdress, and was huddled over an electric fire, shivering.

"Wh-wh-who's there?"

"Ghost Rescue!"

"Oh, w-w-wonderful! I didn't think you'd come!"

"Menhotep?" asked Charlie. "Hang on – you speak English? Then why did you write to us in Egyptian hieroglyphics? We had trouble reading it."

"I'll sh-show you," smiled Menhotep, leading them to a computer. In the glow from the heater they could see it was a very strange computer – the keyboard was hieroglyphic.

"You see? This is the only c-c-computer I can reach, because I can only travel a small d-distance from my coffin. But I have been stuck in this m-m-museum for seventy years – plenty of t-time to learn English!"

"Oh, you poor thing, you're freezing," said Lady F, giving Menhotep her shawl to wear. "Now, how are we going to get you back to Egypt?"

Menhotep took them to his coffin. In the torchlight it shone like the Egyptian sun. Gold! Solid gold, inlaid with blue lapis lazuli, orange carnelian and green jade. There was a golden mask of Menhotep's face with a long curling beard.

"This must be worth millions!" gasped Charlie.

"It means n-n-nothing to me," sniffed Menhotep. "Not without my homeland, my s-sun, my sands, my beautiful River Nile. Break off my b-beard, Charlie, and then you can post it to Egypt, and I can travel with it on the p-p-plane home!"

"Break off your beard?" said Charlie. "But your coffin's so beautiful, it seems terrible to spoil it."

"It's just metal," said Menhotep. "Metal feels nothing. But *I* feel – and I feel cold! Use a chisel, Charlie, and b-break off my beard. Go on, there's nobody to hear you."

Charlie took a hammer and chisel from a drawer, stood over Menhotep's golden face, and took a deep breath. He listened.

"Are you guys sure there's nobody around?"

"Positive, Charlie."

Charlie swung the hammer. Whack!
The chisel bounced off the beard, leaving
a small scratch. The sound echoed around
the hall — whack-ack-ack-ack!

Charlie swung harder. Whack-ack-ack-
ack! He had cut a bigger notch now — but
it was hard work. As the echoes faded
away, Charlie heard something.

"What was that? Sounded like a rumbling."

The ghosts peered out of the windows.

Charlie bit a fingernail. "Do you see anything?"

"It's all right," hissed Florence. "It's just some workmen outside – they've got a digger. Must be doing some work while the museum is closed."

Charlie breathed a sigh of relief – and
carried on hammering.

Whack-ack-ack-ack! Getting there…

Whack-ack-ack-ack! Nearly done it.

Whack-ack-ack-ack! Nearly—

CRASSSSHHHH! The far wall
exploded in a roar of shattering bricks
and a cloud of dust – and a digger came
rumbling in. Several men jumped out.
The ghosts vanished and Charlie hid in a
corner. There, in the shadows, he
listened.

"Where is it, then?" growled a voice. Torches swept round the room, and Charlie curled himself into a ball.

"Wow!" said a second voice. "Would you look at that!"

"Gold!" said a third voice, in a nasty, hungry snarl. "Look how it shines!"

"Shut up, the lot of you!" snapped the first voice. "Get that digger moving!"

With a horrible grinding, scraping noise, the digger scooped up the coffin. All the men climbed aboard, and the digger rumbled back through the hole in the wall and out into the darkness.

Charlie was staring at the hole, dumbfounded, when Menhotep appeared in the middle of it. He looked as if something was tugging him backwards.

"Help me!" he cried. "It's pulling me awayyyyyy…" And suddenly, he was yanked into the night.

Ghost Rescue bundled into the Ghostmobile and gave chase. But where had the coffin-thieves gone?

Rio flew through the starry sky, as high as the Fairfax stone would let him, and turned his sharp eyes to the land below.

"Awwk!" He spotted the digger driving down a narrow lane towards a lonely farmhouse. The farm was high on a hill, above a deep valley with a small village in it. Rio flew after the digger, checking that the Ghostmobile was still below him.

While Lord and Lady F kept their eyes on the road, Florence sat on the roof, never taking her gaze off Rio.

"He's seen them!" she said excitedly. "Take the next left..."

They left the Ghostmobile under a
thicket of bushes and brambles, and spied
on the farm. The digger had been hidden
away in the barn, and now lights were
glowing from the farmhouse. Behind the
curtains they could see silhouettes
moving about.

"Now what do we do?" asked Florence.

"If I can only get to the beard," said Charlie. "It's almost cut through, and I reckon I could snap it off with my hands. Then we can save Menhotep."

"We'll create a diversion," said Lord F. "We'll give them a good spooking – scare them away for long enough for you to sneak in. Come on, Charlie, we'll lead the way. Stay behind us, keep your head down, and when they've run away, grab that beard!"

Suddenly a door opened and light spilled out. There, in the middle of the room, was Menhotep's coffin.

"I'm just going to check on the digger," said one of the men, as he stepped outside – and saw the ghosts.

"AAARRGGHH! GHOSTS!" He backed away and cowered behind the coffin.

"Go away!" shrieked a second man, shrinking into a corner. "Leave us alone!"

But the leader of the gang, whose name was Flynn, stood up, walked over to Lord F, and stared him straight in the face. Lord F howled, and shrieked, and twisted his face every way he could – but Flynn didn't flinch.

"Yeah, that's a very scary face," said
Flynn. "And ooh, that's a terrifying noise.
But tell me, ghost – what can you
actually *do* to me?"

"I can, er…" said Lord F, lost for words. "I can, um… I can boil your blood! And grind your bones!"

"Go on, then," said Flynn. "Boil my blood and grind my bones."

Lord F didn't know what to do. Of course he couldn't do any of those things, and wouldn't want to if he could.

"You see?" Flynn smiled at his mates.
"They can't actually *do* anything to us.
I've come across ghosts before when I've
done museum jobs. They're all mouth, all
'Grrr!' But at the end of the day, they're
just – windbags."

Flynn's face curled into a snarl.
"And now – I'm coming for YOU!
AAARRRRGGGHHHH!"

He charged, and the ghosts were so surprised that they turned and fled out of the farmhouse, into the night. Straight towards Charlie…

"AAARRGGHH!"

Charlie pressed himself flat against the grass and tried to make himself invisible. Heavy boots came stamping towards him, and stopped.

"Well, well, well, what do we have here?"

A strong hand grabbed him and
dragged him up.

"Where did you – ow!"

Charlie bit Flynn's wrist as hard as he
could, and struggled and kicked and
punched.

"You little rat!" yelled Flynn, dragging
Charlie back inside. "This one's a biter."

"What shall we do with him, boss?" asked one of the men. Flynn looked around, and saw the coffin.

"Put him in there," said Flynn with a horrible grin.

"No, please," said Charlie. "I was just out for a walk, please don't put me in there..."

But the men heaved off the golden lid. There, in the coffin, was Menhotep – but not the nice ghost. There was Menhotep the musty, dusty mummy.

"No, please," begged Charlie. "You can't put me in there – with that..."

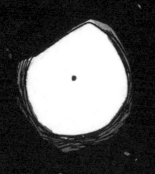

Flynn just grinned, and he shoved
Charlie into the coffin. The lid slid over
him with a horrible grinding noise, and
all was blackness. Charlie could feel
bandages tangling all around him – they
smelled like sweaty socks that had been
left in a locker for four thousand years.
The air was hot and dusty, and Charlie
sneezed. "Aaah-zoozoo!"

"NOOOOOOOO!" he screamed. But no one could hear him. Charlie was all alone.

"What are we going to do?" said Florence. "Charlie can't breathe in there. He'll die!"

"We've got to get help," said her father.

Just then there was a sound in the valley below, the howl of a siren — and they could see a blue flashing light as a police car drove into the village. It parked by the police station.

"The police!" cried Florence. "Hooray! But – how can we get their attention?"

"A siren…" said Lord F, thinking hard.

"What?" said Florence.

"Yes! A siren! We'll make ourselves
into a siren. Come on, down the hill,
as far as we can go. There, the police
station is right below us. They'll look out
of the window and see, if we give them
something to see…and hear.
Come on everyone, huddle together,
and make yourselves blue and bright…
Concentrate! Charlie's life depends on
us…"

Charlie was losing his temper. The dust tickled his nose and stung his eyes, and the bandages seemed to be wrapping him tighter and tighter. The coffin smelled like a wrestler's armpit. Charlie pounded at the coffin lid until his hands were sore – but it was much too heavy.

"Aaah-zoozoo!" sneezed Charlie. "I can't move, I can't see, I can't breathe and I can't stand it anymore – GET ME OUT OF HERE!"

"Charlie!" said a voice.

"Who...who's that?"

"It's me, Menhotep! I'm here. Don't be afraid."

"Who's going to open this lid?" snapped Charlie. "*You*? If not, WHO?"

"Your friends have got a clever idea, Charlie. They're calling the police. They'll be here soon."

The Fairfaxes concentrated, and grew brighter and brighter still. Now they were a dazzling light, casting a blue glow over the hillside.

"Now…" said Lord F. "HOWL!"

"WWWOOOOOHHHHHHHHHH HHHOOOOOOO!"

"WWWOOOOOOHHHHHHHHHH HHHHOOOOOO!"

"What's that noise?" said Police
Constable Carter, looking up from his
coffee in the police station.

"That's a siren," said Sergeant Petrie.
"Sounds like it's coming from up the hill.
Look, up there! Quick, Carter, sound the
alarm. Call all units!"

Soon two police cars and a police van were driving up the hill, lights flashing and sirens howling.

"It's the cops!" cried Flynn. "Quick, get the digger!"

Charlie could see nothing, but he could hear shouts and bangs and crashes.

"Menhotep! What's going on?"

"The police are here, Charlie!" said Menhotep. "Two cars and a van – and the robbers are making a run for the digger. Flynn's driving – here it c-c-comes!"

SMASH!

"What was that?"
asked Charlie.

"Flynn's smashed through the wall.
He's coming for us. He's coming for the
coffin!"

Flynn lowered the scoop, slid it under
the coffin, and picked it up.

"You're under arrest!" cried Sergeant Petrie. "Turn off your engine right now!"

"Try to stop me, copper!" yelled Flynn. "Ha, ha, ha!" The digger came crashing out of what was left of the farmhouse and, with the coffin, went speeding off – straight into the police van.

CRASH!

Charlie's world turned upside down.
Everything was spinning, roaring
madness.

"HEEELLLPPP!" he shrieked.
Suddenly the coffin came apart and
Charlie went flying through the air –
and landed with a thud on the grass.

Everything was chaos – flashing lights,
rumbling engines, spinning tyres, cars
and van and digger, police running and
shouting, robbers trying to get away.

Nobody even noticed Charlie. Aching all over, gulping in the cool sweet air, he crawled away to hide. His hand fell upon a small object, and without thinking, he took it with him to a clump of bushes. Only when he was safely in the shadows did Charlie look in his hand.

The beard! The beard from the coffin's chin!

"Charlie!" said Menhotep, appearing beside him. "You've done it! I'm f-f-free!"

Soon it was all over. Flynn and his gang struggled and fought and tried to run away. But it was not long before Sergeant Petrie and his men had them handcuffed and sitting in the back of the bashed and battered police van. Nobody saw the pizza van driving slowly away – a pizza van with a boy, a beard, and *six* ghosts, one much, much older than the others...

Two weeks later, Charlie and the Fairfaxes were gathered round the computer screen to read an email.

YOU HAVE EMAIL

Dear Charlie and friends,

Greetings from Egypt! The beard that you posted, Charlie, has arrived safely – here in the Valley of the Kings. I'm home. I'm happy. I'm warm! Thank you so much, every one of you – I'd never have got here without you. Long live Ghost Rescue! If you ever need any help from the land of the pharaohs, you know where I am.

Your friend

Menhotep

"Hooray!" cried Florence.

"Woof, woof!" barked Zanzibar.

"Long live Ghost Rescue, indeed!" laughed Charlie.

WRITTEN BY
## Andrew Murray

ILLUSTRATED BY
## Sarah Horne

All priced at £8.99

The Ghost Rescue books are available from all good bookshops,
or can be ordered direct from the publisher:
Orchard Books, PO BOX 29, Douglas IM99 1BQ
Credit card orders please telephone 01624 836000
or fax 01624 837033 or visit our website: www.orchardbooks.co.uk
or email: bookshop@enterprise.net for details.

To order please quote title, author and ISBN
and your full name and address.
Cheques and postal orders should be made payable to 'Bookpost plc'.
Postage and packing is FREE within the UK
(overseas customers should add £1.00 per book).

Prices and availability are subject to change.